For Chloe Grace —ADP

To my little sister, Ann —DM

About This Book

The illustrations for this book were created using a mixture of traditional 2D painting and digital drawing and painting. This book was edited by Farrin Jacobs and Erika Turner and designed by Tracy Shaw. The production was supervised by Nyamekye Waliyaya, and the production editor was Jen Graham. The text was set in Aleo, and the display type is King & Queen.

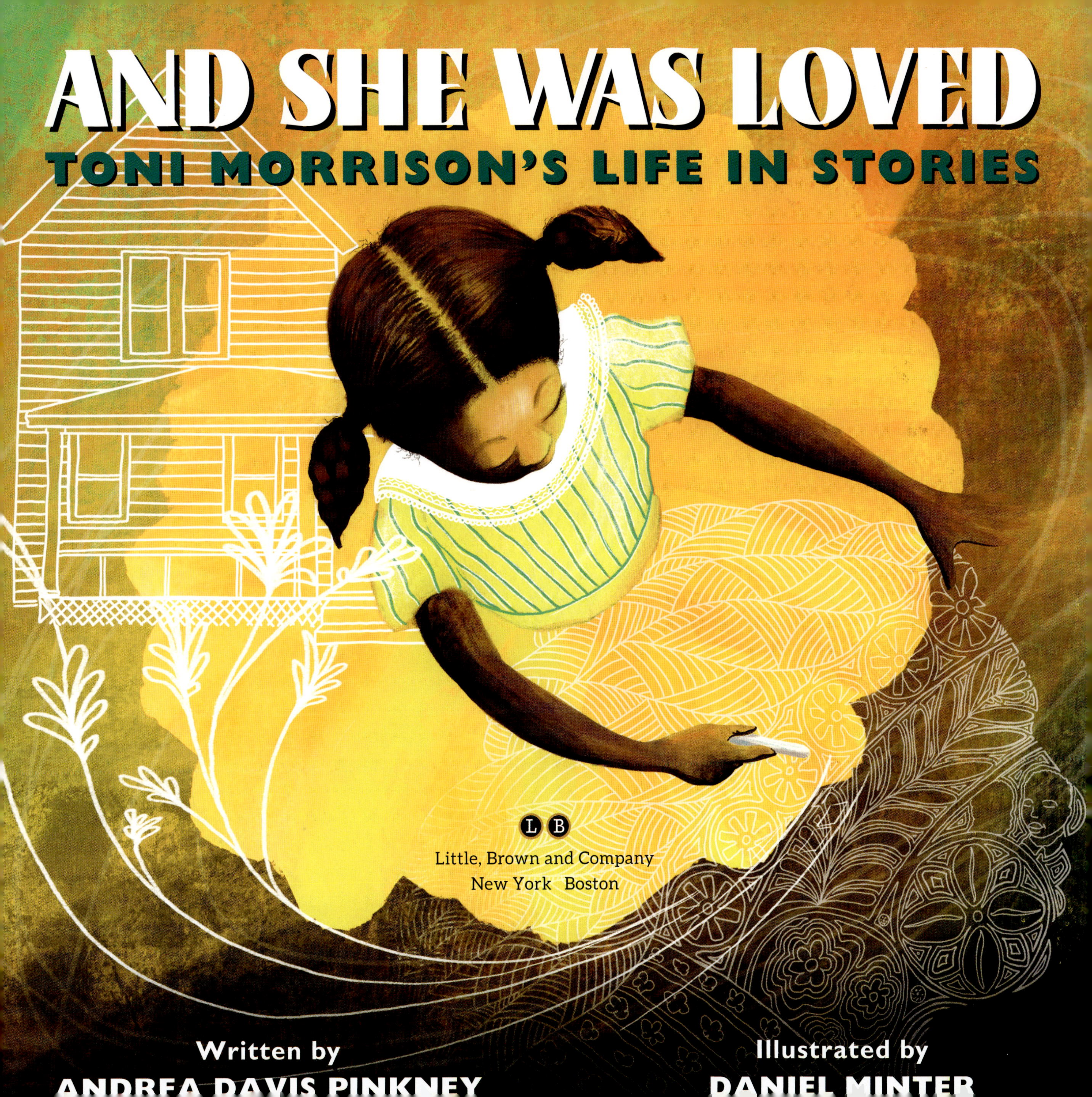

AND SHE WAS LOVED

TONI MORRISON'S LIFE IN STORIES

LB

Little, Brown and Company

New York Boston

Written by

ANDREA DAVIS PINKNEY

Illustrated by

DANIEL MINTER

Oh, *Toni Morrison*, do you feel it?
Your love has lifted us to places untouched.
You, born with a roar for stories that speak.

And she was loved . . .

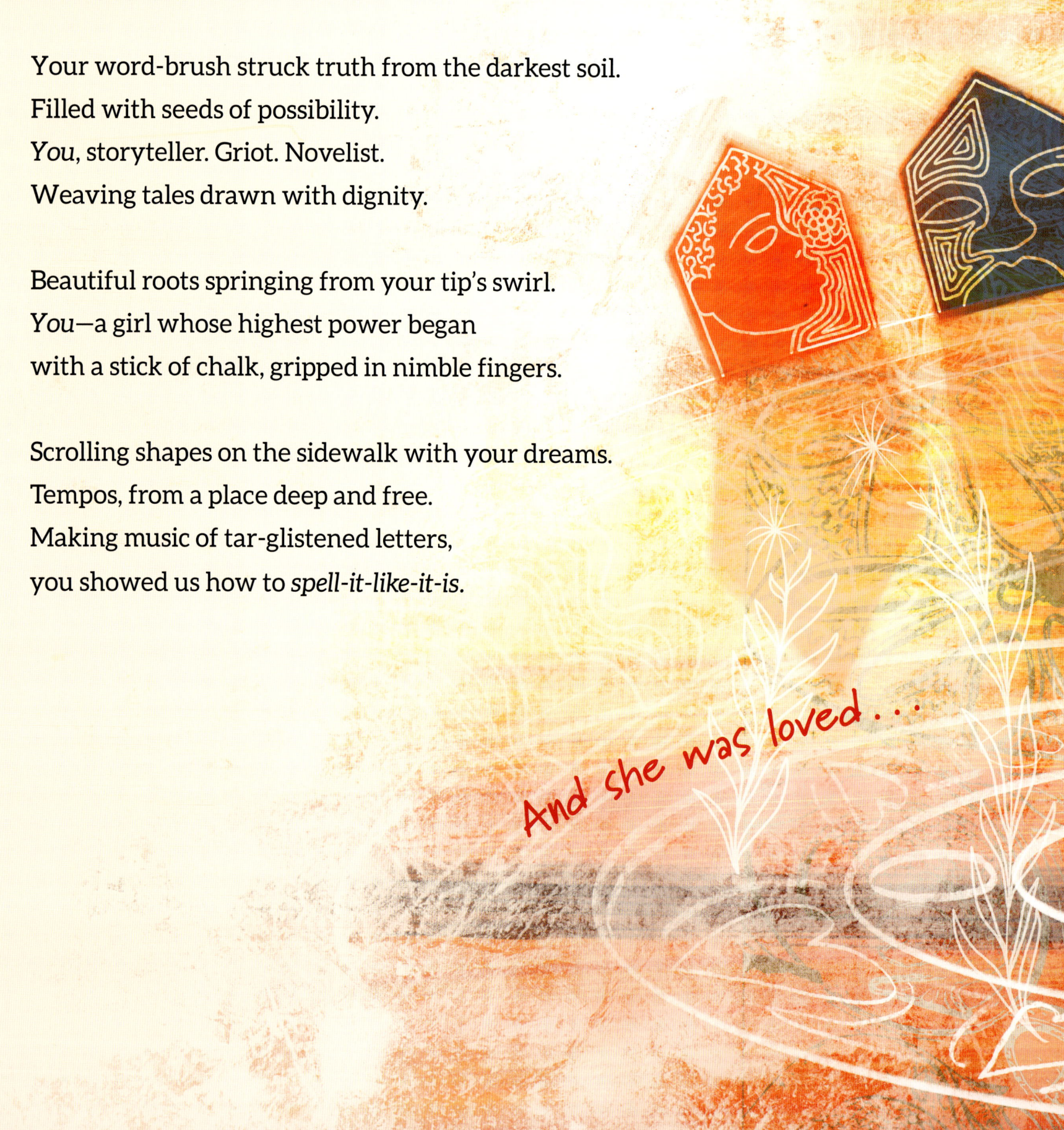

Your word-brush struck truth from the darkest soil.
Filled with seeds of possibility.
You, storyteller. Griot. Novelist.
Weaving tales drawn with dignity.

Beautiful roots springing from your tip's swirl.
You—a girl whose highest power began
with a stick of chalk, gripped in nimble fingers.

Scrolling shapes on the sidewalk with your dreams.
Tempos, from a place deep and free.
Making music of tar-glistened letters,
you showed us how to *spell-it-like-it-is*.

And she was loved . . .

You, little girl, adored by the sky's dawning light, as you flew into this world.
Eyes bright. Gaze straight on. Seeing.

Lorain, Ohio, is the birthplace that embraced you in its cradle.
Chloe Ardelia, the second of four children, born to Ramah and George Wofford,
your mother and father who blessed you with that radiant name.
"Blooming floret," it means.

Yes, child, you blossomed.
Chloe A., as bright as Ohio's state flower.
A red carnation, imagination bursting.
Birthright rising.

Townsfolk spoke of your house on Elyria Avenue.
Called it *that tired gray lady*, for its sunken front porch and crooked clapboards.

Inside its rickety kitchen, folktales and spirituals bubbled over,
misting the windows, boiling up your affection for letters.

And she was loved . . .

You—at school, the only Black girl in your first-grade class.
You—the gifted student who could read before anyone else.
You—Chloe, one and only.

Words, and their power, became your friends,
reaching out, embracing, inviting you to their party.

On the street signs—*words*.
At church—*words*.
In your family Bible—*words*.

Jump-rope poems with your sister, Lois,
twirling rhymes, fast and free.

Hopscotch harmonies leaped from your teenaged feet
as you taught your little brothers, Raymond and George,
how to crack the code on their *ABC*s.

And she was loved...

Years later, you proclaim: *Hello, Howard University!*
When that college calls your name, you answer back.
Say—*Here I am.*

At Howard, you shake hands with reflections of yourself.
And you change your name.

Nice to meet you. I'm Toni.

You greet other Colored kids from Podunk places,
eager to step into their own smartness.
Free to explore what it means to be Black
on a campus planted with *We, Us, Ours*.
You are now among others who know how it feels
to peel small-town thinking wide open.

Right there, each student claims it.
My Howard U.
Ours—as in, for Black folks.
We—as in, HBCU.
Us—as in, togetherhood.

With your college degree in hand,

here comes a golden seed, planted in your ready palm.

Toni Morrison, sign here, you're hired.

They know you're smart when they let you in

but have no idea you will build empires.

Yes, you sign.

Sow your own dotted line.

Seed planter, pressing possibilities into what others see as brittle dirt.

Tell the doubters to step back. *Watch me work.*

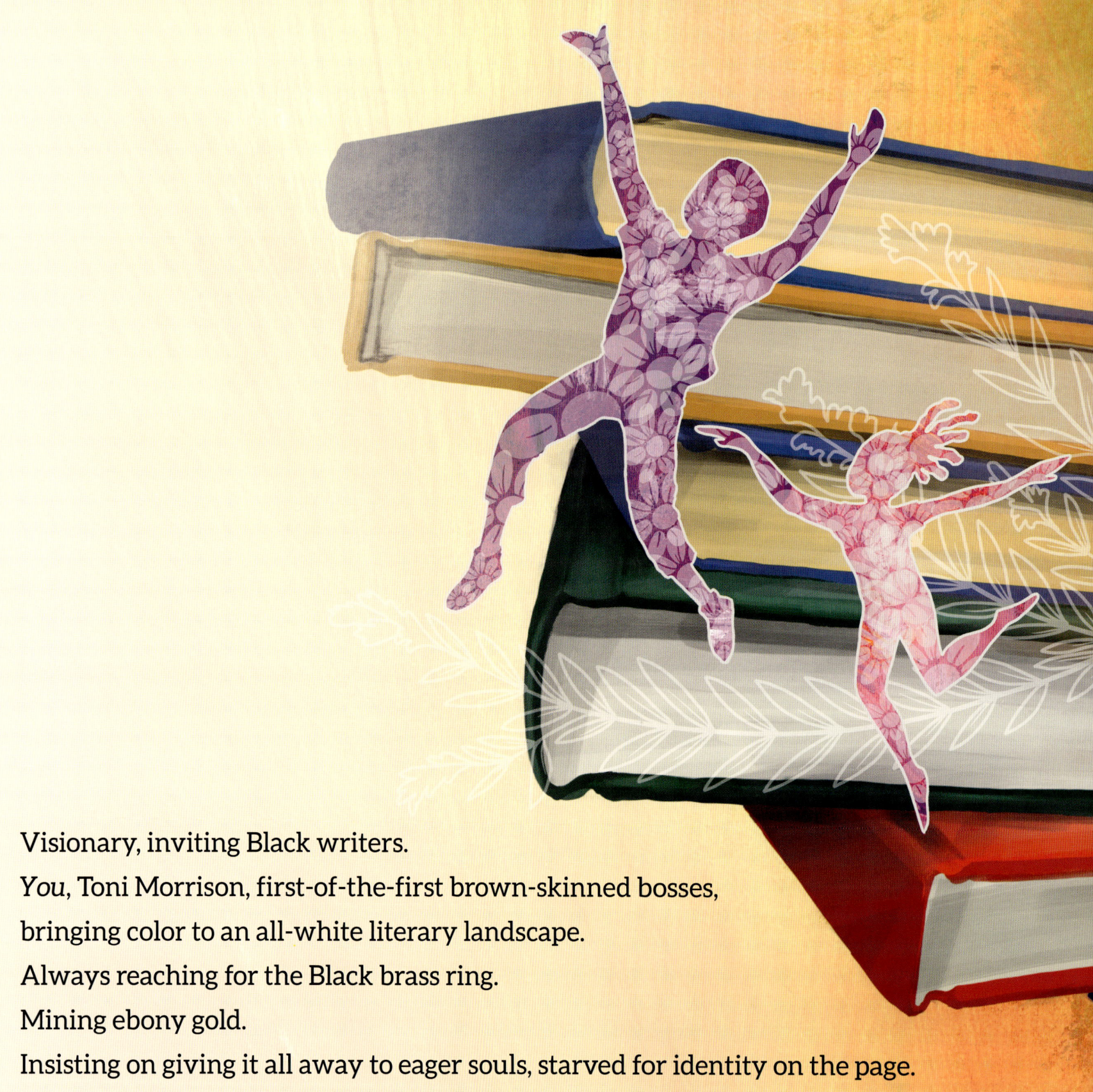

Visionary, inviting Black writers.

You, Toni Morrison, first-of-the-first brown-skinned bosses,

bringing color to an all-white literary landscape.

Always reaching for the Black brass ring.

Mining ebony gold.

Insisting on giving it all away to eager souls, starved for identity on the page.

Oh, Toni Morrison, you ignite proud Black literary light.

And she was loved . . .

Alright, now—here's a secret that only gets told when you dare to share it:

Your planting and tilling are filled with self-tending, too.

Yes, that's *you*, up at four in the morning.

Dawning writer, breaking quiet soil on your own stories, but—*shhhh*—

not telling a soul.

You work before the *dew* even knows what to *do*.

You craft Fine Blackness at daybreak.

Blue-lined yellow tablet, pen in your hand.

Whispering words onto pages while your babies stretch in their beds.

Rush-write before Mama Muse slips away.

You manage a scribbled story

about a Black girl wishing for sapphire eyes.

With her tale, your own writing bursts fully alive.

At the same time, everybody's pulling at you—yanking at your limbs and wits.

You—head of household, raising kids alone.

You—a working mother with the might of ten men.

You—cook meals, pack school lunches, shape your boys' 'fros, *and* shape prose.

You—edit stories by other writers to bring home the bacon
that sizzles on the griddle as the sun says hello to another nonstop day.

And she was loved...

You, Toni Morrison, stay the course.

Bringing the beauty of dark truth with your own tale to tell.

You, Toni Morrison, probe that hidden nook.

Force us to look.

Make us gaze into the Bluest Eye.

We can't glance away from that misguided girl.

Blue-black child bitten by the dogs of self-doubt.

Your debut novel stares down self-hatred, doesn't blink once.

The Bluest Eye, inspired by your own Lorain, Ohio, childhood.

Oh, Toni Morrison, your story sews self-love into so many souls.

You stitch a clear-eyed vision by encouraging us to:

Speak up.

Be strong.

Deny the blond-dolly lie.

And she was loved . . .

Soon, more stories rise.

Oh, Toni Morrison—outspoken sparrow.

Speckle-flecked wings alight, flying so high.

You—setting the sky on fire. Free-spirited storyteller.

Toni Morrison, you help us soar up . . . up . . . up . . . through sacred pages.

Rising past this world's ugly ways.

Your writing—

    fanciful . . .

    exuberant . . .

    dazzling . . .

    real . . .

Oh, Toni Morrison, you liberate all of us.

You—let us breathe.

And she was loved!

Oh, Toni Morrison, you give us freedom's flight.

    A brilliant mix of:

gutbucket rhythms

                           roots

call-and-response word-music

                                    fervor

            oral histories

            laments

                    traditions

        legacies.

And to keep us on the way, here comes that chorus of *Alright, then!*

Toni Morrison, you do not shy back.
You—mother of spiritual mythology.
You—deliver the ticket. Finally. A front-row seat to *Black-is-truly-beautiful.*

For lifting us to a higher vision,
awards, medals, honors arrive.
Ohio child, brown-skinned girl, now grown,
the time comes to greet your becoming.
To step up to your golden nobility:
recognized, seen, unveiled from the shadows.

Pulitzer.

     Nobel.

        Presidential Medal.

And she was loved . . .

But the true prizes live in the eyes you've opened.
Wide possibility, shining Black pride.
Your stitchwork, a quilt of unspooled stories.

Your writing:
sparks
reveals
matters
endures.

Your language translates humanity,
uttered in every tongue.

Oh, Toni Morrison . . .
Your prose—a tapestry of truths,
superstition,
strut.

Your word-music
taking us to unpaved places.

Your scats and swings,
rooted in oral tradition.

And she was loved . . .

You—craft-messenger.
You—box-braider, weaving:
Black pride
Black joy
Black families
Blackness.

Today, we rejoice in that woven plait.

Oh, Toni Morrison, your griot grit puts the words in our hands.

Says: *It's your turn to write a self-love letter.*

Says: *The authorship is your heart's true wish.*

Says: *You, reader, can be the writer, too.*

Says: *Look in the mirror.*

Says: *Open the window.*

Says: *Turn your face to the sun kissing your cheeks.*

Shouts: *I am LOVED! I am loved! I am loved!*

Oh, Toni Morrison, we exclaim your name.

YOU are loved!

Toni Morrison, thank you for granting us bold permission.

Thank you for the up-nod that says *Go 'head.*

Thank you for affirming:

Now, child, invite your imagination!

Dear one, dream with wide-open eyes.

When a stick of chalk fills your fingers.

When Mama Muse visits you at twilight.

When all you want to do is write, write, write.

Make your mark on the tar.

Stitch your story.

You are . . .

HOW THIS POEM CAME TO BE

The search for love and identity runs through most everything I write. —Toni Morrison

This narrative is a love letter to an outspoken sparrow who transformed lives through her storytelling.

When you're a Black girl who tumbles into this world with a snare in your throat, you spend your days looking for ways to set your voice free. That was me. I was a child who struggled in school, often because the books on my classroom reading lists had very little to do with my Black experience.

Then, like a glistening key that unlocked my soul's need to see myself, Toni Morrison's storytelling came into my life. It didn't matter that her books had themes too complex for my childhood understanding. The cover of Toni Morrison's first novel, *The Bluest Eye*, drew me in like a new friend I couldn't wait to know better. The book's jacket was impossible to ignore. It showed the story's main character, Pecola, a Black girl, embracing a white doll. That arresting image depicted the pain of what I would later come to identify as a condition I call "anxious apartness"—the queasy gnashing I experienced as the only Black girl in most of my school classes. Anxious apartness made me believe I was on the fringes, unseen, and that, like a bird stuck inside a gated cage, my voice was locked inside the lie that tried to tell me I was insignificant.

Fortunately, my parents and extended family loved me enough to soften these harsh feelings. Also fortunate was the fact that Black literature filled the bookshelves of our home.

As an author who spends time with students all over the world, I meet kids who are aspiring writers. These young people are eager to know more about Toni Morrison's storytelling gifts.

The power of love is the enduring thematic thread woven throughout Ms. Morrison's books. This spoke to me as a young reader embarking upon her stories. Oprah Winfrey says, "Toni Morrison's work shows us, through pain, all the myriad ways we can come to love." Toni Morrison's literary canon and Oprah's wisdom are the seeds that inspired this book's creation and title.

And She Was Loved is drawn from a declaration made in Ms. Morrison's *Song of Solomon*. When Pilate, one of the novel's central characters, calls out, "And she was loved!" she's railing against a society that allows hatred of Black people to persist. At the same time, Pilate is pronouncing love's infinite power; thus, the echoed refrain that is whispered throughout this book's narrative—*And she was loved . . . And she was loved . . .*—is symbolic of Ms. Morrison's body of work.

—Andrea Davis Pinkney

ARTIST'S NOTE

Toni Morrison, for real?

Your words have been inspirational in shaping my way of thinking about my artwork for years, so anything I have to say about you can begin with a look back to any of my previous paintings. From you, I learned that the characters I love don't have to be good or virtuous people. Their simple existence affirms our many possibilities as humans.

In the illustrations created for *And She Was Loved*, I painted the reality that you are always with us. First, with a wash color on watercolor paper, seeking a blend of yellow and orange textures that would catch your eye and match your glow. The goddess Oshun would approve of the golden hues and the vibrant greens.

After the surface treatment of acrylic wash, I added a primary figure that reflects some aspect of the narrative. One of the special things about working on this book is that I have been calling it a "praise poem" for you, Toni Morrison. While some of the images represent different stages in your life, I wanted to include the spiritual presence of your full self and the powerful ancestor you have become.

Toni, look closely at the lines, because some of them might resemble characters that could have lived in your novels. The white lines of flowers, figures, shapes, and textures create a veil that does not hide but reveals the lasting impact of your words.

Though many of the backgrounds and images are hand-painted, I used a computer to compose and layer the final illustrations. The lines are, for me, a form of meditation that highlights the poetry of Andrea Davis Pinkney's words, while also reflecting my praise for you.

With love,
Daniel

Dwight Carter

Toni Morrison revolutionized the world of literary storytelling. Her narratives are rooted in history, mythology, spirituality, and song. In addition to her work as an editor and novelist, Ms. Morrison wrote an opera, crafted many essays about race and Black identity, and curated an exhibition at the Louvre Museum in Paris. From 1989 until her retirement in 2006, she served as the Robert F. Goheen Chair in the Humanities at Princeton University, where she taught an emerging generation of writers and thinkers.

TONI MORRISON TIMELINE

1931. Chloe Ardelia Wofford is born on February 18. She later changes her name to Toni Morrison.

1949. She enrolls in Howard University, a Historically Black College, where she joins a group of poets and writers who meet weekly to share their work. She becomes a member of the drama club, where, through the theatrical form, she discovers the power of characterization and dialogue. Toni graduates in 1953 with an English degree, then goes on to Cornell University to earn a master of arts in 1955.

1958. Toni marries Harold Morrison. They have two sons, Ford and Slade. After their divorce, Toni retains custody of her boys. She keeps her married name: *Toni Morrison.*

1967. Ms. Morrison becomes the first woman of color in a senior role at the Random House publishing company, where she flings open the door for Black talent. She welcomes Angela Davis, Chinua Achebe, Huey P. Newton, and Gayl Jones to the fold. She also publishes a book by Muhammad Ali, and like him, Toni Morrison is floating like a butterfly and becoming the greatest.

1970. *The Bluest Eye*, her debut novel, is crafted from a short story she wrote while attending a writer's group when she was teaching at Howard. In the book, set in Lorain, Ohio, where Toni grew up, the main character, a Black girl named Pecola, is bullied because of her dark skin color. More than anything, Pecola wishes she had blue eyes, blond hair, and white skin.

1977. *Song of Solomon* is published. It's said to be Toni Morrison's most ambitious novel, a mix of historical fiction and magical realism that explores what it means for a person's soul to rise past the evil traps of racism and oppression. Some say the voices and plights reflected in *Song of Solomon*'s characters embody the power of the Black Lives Matter movement.

1987. Ms. Morrison's *Beloved* explores the horrors of slavery and racial violence. The novel is based on a real event Toni Morrison reads about and turns into a gripping work of fiction, hailed as her masterwork. It's set after the Civil War, when a family is haunted by a ghostly presence in their Ohio home.

1988. *Beloved* wins the Pulitzer Prize for fiction.

1993. Ms. Morrison is the first African American woman to win the Nobel Prize in Literature, an honor bestowed after many fellow writers speak out, claiming her time has come. Her books are published across the globe.

1997. *Paradise* is Toni Morrison's first novel after winning the Nobel Prize. It completes what has been called the Beloved trilogy, books centered in Black history, culture, and humanity. *Beloved*, *Jazz*, and *Paradise* comprise the trilogy. *Paradise* illuminates the fickle nature of romance, the power of inner resolve, and the strength of women who don't back down to the misdeeds of men.

2012. President Barack Obama honors her with the Presidential Medal of Freedom.

2019. Toni Morrison passes away on August 5, leaving a profound legacy woven with myth, magic, superstition, and truth.

The author wishes to thank the Toni Morrison Society for their ongoing work in illuminating the life and legacy of this visionary genius, and for inspiring this book through their many lectures, discussions, and research materials.

SELECTED WORKS OF TONI MORRISON

The Bluest Eye (1970)

Sula (1973)

Song of Solomon (1977)

Tar Baby (1981)

Beloved (1987)

Jazz (1992)

Paradise (1997)

Love (2003)

A Mercy (2008)

Home (2012)

God Help the Child (2015)

Children's Books

Remember: The Journey to School Integration (2004)

Written with Slade Morrison:

The Big Box (1999)

The Book of Mean People (2002)

Who's Got Game? The Ant or the Grasshopper? (2003), *The Lion or the Mouse?* (2003),

Poppy or the Snake? (2004)

Peeny Butter Fudge (2009)

Little Cloud and Lady Wind (2010)

Please, Louise (2014)

SOURCES CONSULTED FOR THE CREATION OF THIS BOOK

Nonfiction Books

Morrison, Toni. *The Measure of Our Lives: A Gathering of Wisdom*. New York: Alfred A. Knopf, 2019.

Morrison, Toni. *The Origin of Others*. Cambridge, Massachusetts: Harvard University Press, 2017.

Morrison, Toni. *Playing in the Dark: Whiteness and the Literary Imagination*. Cambridge, Massachusetts: Harvard University Press, 1992.

Micucci, Dana. "An Inspired Life: Toni Morrison Writes and a Generation Listens." In *Conversations with Toni Morrison*, edited by Danille Taylor-Guthrie. Jackson: University Press of Mississippi, 1994.

Film

Greenfield-Sanders, Timothy, dir. *Toni Morrison: The Pieces I Am*. Documentary. New York: Magnolia Pictures, 2019.

Articles

Als, Hilton. "Toni Morrison's Truth." *New Yorker*, August 8, 2019.

Chambers, Veronica. "The Essential Toni Morrison." *New York Times*, February 18, 2021.

Hoby, Hermione. "Toni Morrison: 'I'm writing for Black people . . . I don't have to apologise.'" *Guardian*, April 25, 2015.

Schappell, Elissa, and Claudia Brodsky Lacour. "Toni Morrison: The Art of Fiction No. 134." Interview. *Paris Review*, Issue 128, Fall 1993.

Broadcast Interviews

60 Minutes Overtime with Ed Bradley, March 8, 1998.

"'I Regret Everything': Toni Morrison Looks Back on Her Personal Life." NPR's *Fresh Air*, April 20, 2015.

"In Depth: Toni Morrison." C-SPAN, February 4, 2001.

"Toni Morrison on a Writer's Life." *CBS Sunday Morning*, April 4, 2004.

"Toni Morrison, Novelist, Editor." Conference on Literature and the Urban Experience, 1980.

Websites

Cultural Front. "Legacy Work, the Toni Morrison Society, and Thornwillow Press." June 16, 2021. https://www.culturalfront.org/2021/06/legacy-work-toni-morrison-and.html.

The Toni Morrison Society. https://www.tonimorrisonsociety.org.

Quotes

36   "The search for love": Micucci, "An Inspired Life."

36   "Toni Morrison's work shows us": Greenfield-Sanders, dir., *Toni Morrison: The Pieces I Am*.